A Kooties Club MYSTERY

Membership Card

Name

Nickname

School

Age

The Mystery
of I L♥ve Elvis

by M. J. Cosson

Perfection Learning® CA

Cover and Inside Illustrations: Michael A. Aspengren

For information, contact
Perfection Learning® Corporation,
1000 North Second Avenue, P.O. Box 500,
Logan, Iowa 51545-0500.
perfectionlearning.com
PB ISBN-10: 0-7891-2300-2 ISBN-13: 978-0-7891-2300-8
RLB ISBN-10: 0-7807-7268-7 ISBN-13: 978-0-7807-7268-7

8 9 10 11 12 13 PP 13 12 11 10 09 08

Table of Contents

Introduction

Abe, Ben, Gabe, Toby, and Ty live in a large city. There isn't much for kids to do. There isn't even a park close by.

Their neighborhood is made up of
apartment houses and trailer parks.
Gas stations and small shops stand
where the parks and grass used to be.
And there aren't many houses with
big yards.

Ty and Abe live in an apartment complex. Next door is a large vacant lot. It is full of brush, weeds, and trash. A path runs across the lot. On the other side is a trailer park. Ben and Toby live there.

Across the street from the trailer park is a big gray house. Gabe lives in the top apartment of the house.

The five boys have known each other since they started school. But they haven't always been friends.

The other kids say the boys have cooties. And the other kids won't touch them with a ten-foot pole. So Abe, Ben, Gabe, Toby, and Ty have formed their own club. They call it the Kooties Club.

Here's how to join. If no one else will have anything to do with you, you're in.

The boys call themselves the Koots for short. Ben's grandma calls his grandpa an *old coot.* And Ben thinks his grandpa is pretty cool. So if he's an old coot, Ben and his friends must be young koots.

The Koots play ball and hang out with each other. But most of all, they look for mysteries to solve.

Chapter 1

The Signs

"That's three," said Ben. "There's one by the trailer park sign. There's one by the Purdy's trailer. And this one."

It was Saturday morning. Ben and Toby stood on the sidewalk in front of the trailer park. Toby got down on his hands and knees. He wanted to get a better look.

"They used dark pink chalk for the heart," Toby said. "And they filled it in. The letters are very good. They drew around the heart with light pink chalk. And they drew around each letter with blue chalk. I don't think a kid did this."

Just then, Abe, Ty, and Gabe walked up. All five members of the Kooties Club looked at the sidewalk.

"What's up?" asked Ty. He looked at the sidewalk. "You have these too?"

"Yeah," said Toby. "Do you have them at the apartments?"

"Yeah," said Ty.

"They're all over," said Gabe. "I even have them in front of my house."

11

"I guess somebody really likes those little pixies," said Abe.

"What?" asked all the other Koots. They gave Abe a puzzled look.

"Aren't they elves? Little pixies?" he asked.

"No, Abe. This says E-L-V-I-S. Elvis. Not elves," said Toby. He shook his head.

"What is an Elvis?" asked Abe.

Gabe explained, "Not a what. A who. He was the king of rock and roll. He lived before we were born. Sometimes you hear his songs on the oldies station."

Ty was glad Abe had asked. He didn't know who or what Elvis was either. But he didn't want to ask.

"Yeah," said Toby. "He played a guitar. And he combed his hair back like this." Toby used his hands to show how Elvis wore his hair.

"And he danced like this," said Gabe. He wiggled his hips.

Gabe went on. "I think he still has a fan club somewhere. I saw something on TV about him."

"I saw that too," said Toby.

"So what is all this?" asked Ty. "This stuff just popped up overnight. It's pretty strange. And why is there a heart instead of an *o* in the word *love?*"

"The heart means love," explained Gabe. "My sisters write that all the time."

"Must be a big fan," said Ben.

"I wonder who it is," said Gabe.

"Let's check it out," said Ty.

"Wow! Another mystery!" said Toby.

Chapter 2

A Big Fan

The Koots walked around the neighborhood. They looked for I L♥ve Elvis signs. They found nine.

They came back to the sidewalk where they had started.

"I think the same person did them all," said Toby. "It must have taken her all night."

"Why do you think it's a her?" asked Ben.

"Because Elvis was a guy," Toby explained. "No guy's going to write I L♥ve Elvis. Maybe I Like Elvis. But not I L♥ve Elvis."

"Oh, yeah," said Ben. "That makes sense."

"But why would someone spend all night writing I L♥ve Elvis?" asked Ty.

"Fans are strange. They do funny things to show they like someone. We may be dealing with a real nutcase," answered Gabe. "My sisters are nuts. But even **they** wouldn't do this."

"Let's see what clues we have so far," said Ben. "We know the person did this last night."

16

"We think the person lives around here," said Ty.

"We think the person is a girl," added Ben.

"We know the person loves Elvis," said Gabe.

"We know she used chalk. And we know she is a good writer!" shouted Abe.

"Any guesses?" asked Ty.

Just then, Mrs. Purdy drove past. Her car top was down. Rock and roll music blasted from her radio.

She waved to the Koots. Her ponytail bobbed in time to the music.

"Mrs. Purdy!" yelled Toby. "She loves rock and roll!"

"Yeah!" said Ben. "One time I saw her and Mr. Purdy dressed up for a party. She had on a big, full skirt. It had a poodle on it. And Mr. Purdy was dressed like Elvis. He had his hair combed back. He had on a shiny shirt and carried a guitar."

"Mrs. Purdy!" shouted the Koots. "Let's check her out!"

Chapter 3

The King of Rock and Roll

By noon, the Koots had set up a stakeout near Mrs. Purdy's trailer.

They played hackey-sack. They weren't very good at the game. The hackey-sack kept flying away.

At last, Mrs. Purdy returned. She parked her car and hopped out. She walked toward her trailer. She had some bags in her arms. The Koots ran to her.

"Can we help you?" they asked.

"Sure, boys. There's more in the car," Mrs. Purdy said.

Each boy grabbed a bag. They carried them into Mrs. Purdy's trailer. A picture of Elvis hung on the wall above the couch. It was painted on soft, black cloth. The Koots looked at it and smiled.

"So," said Ty. "I guess you love Elvis."

"Yes, I do," said Mrs. Purdy. "He was the king of rock and roll. And I love rock and roll."

She stopped for a minute. She looked at the boys. "But I wonder who else loves Elvis," she said.

"What do you mean?" asked Ben.

"Didn't you see?" asked Mrs. Purdy. "Someone wrote I L♥ve Elvis right outside my trailer. It was a nice gift. I don't know who it's from. But I'd sure like to find out."

The Kooties looked at each other.

"We thought you did it," said Gabe.

"Oh my," said Mrs. Purdy. "I **do** love Elvis. But I couldn't spend all that time on my knees. Not even for him. I think a much younger person did it."

"When did you first notice it?" asked Toby.

"Just this morning. I let out my little dog, Elvis. And there it was."

"Do you think Mr. Purdy did it?" asked Ben.

21

"Oh my, no," said Mrs. Purdy. "I asked him to dress up like Elvis for a party once. You'd have thought I'd asked for the moon. He's not a big fan."

"Maybe he did it for you. Is it your birthday?" asked Abe.

"No, dear," answered Mrs. Purdy. She shook her head and laughed.

"Maybe Elvis did it," Mrs. Purdy added. "You know, some people think he's still alive."

"Do you think so?" asked Abe.

"I'm sure Elvis is dead," said Mrs. Purdy. "But there are many look-alikes. I can see why some people think so."

"What do you mean *look-alike?*" asked Abe.

"Someone who dresses like Elvis and pretends to be him," said Mrs. Purdy.

"Maybe a look-alike did it," said Gabe. "There are eight more I L♥ve Elvis signs just like that one."

"Eight more!" said Mrs. Purdy. "I want to meet this artist!"

Mrs. Purdy reached into a sack. She pulled out a box of doughnuts. She gave one to each boy.

"Thanks for your help, boys," she said. "Please let me know if you find out who else loves Elvis."

Chapter 4

The Stakeouts

Once outside, Ben said, "Now we're back to square one."

"I still think Mrs. Purdy did it," said Ty. "She just doesn't want us to know. Who could love Elvis more than she does? She even named her dog Elvis."

"I don't think so," said Toby. "She might write it once. But not nine times. I think this was done by a group."

"A fan club," said Gabe. "A weirdo fan club."

"I have an idea," said Abe. "Let's each stake out one of the I L♥ve Elvis signs. Maybe whoever did it will return to the scene of the crime."

"Not a bad idea, Sherlock," said Ben. "We'll ask Mrs. Purdy to watch too. She'll tell us if she sees anything. We can cover the rest. Some of them are close together."

For the rest of the day, the Koots staked out the I L♥ve Elvis signs. The boys stood close enough to see. But they weren't close enough to be seen.

Toby read a book. Ben had two comic books. Ty bounced a ball. Abe played with the hackey-sack. And Gabe just sat and thought. He was forming a plan.

People walked by. Once in a while, someone stopped and read an I L♥ve Elvis sign. Some people laughed. But nobody acted funny. And nobody had any chalk. No clues that afternoon.

The boys spent Sunday looking for clues too. Besides Mrs. Purdy, they didn't know anyone who really loved Elvis. The mystery was driving them nuts.

Chapter 5

The Note

Monday morning, Gabe sat in class. It was silent reading time. He was reading a book. All of a sudden, a note landed on his book. Gabe looked to see where it came from.

Pam was looking at him. She had a big frown on her face. He looked the other way. Jade was frowning at him too.

Gabe picked up the note. He put it in his pocket. Pam got up to sharpen her pencil. As she passed Gabe, she stuck out her hand.

"Give me that," she whispered.

Gabe acted like he didn't hear her.

Later at lunch, Pam came up to Gabe.

"Give me the note," she said.

"What note?" asked Gabe. "I don't know what you're talking about."

"I'll get you for this," said Pam. "Boy, will you be sorry."

Pam walked over to the table where Anna, Jamie, Jade, and Sara sat. Pam said something to them. They looked at Gabe. They all had frowns on their faces.

28

Gabe just smiled and waved. He walked away.

Gabe didn't have a chance to read the note until after school. He didn't want the teacher to catch him with some girl's note. He read the note. Here's what it said:

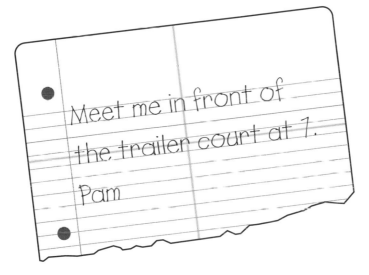

Meet me in front of
the trailer court at 7.
Pam

Gabe was so excited. A clue! Why would Pam want to meet her friends in front of the trailer court? I L♥ve Elvis was there!

Gabe decided not to tell the other Koots about the note yet. If they all showed up, the girls wouldn't come. Besides, Gabe kind of liked Pam. But he didn't want anybody to know. Most of all, not Pam.

At 6:45, Gabe hid in some bushes in front of the trailer court. He was close to the I L♥ve Elvis sign. Gabe sat in the bushes for almost an hour. The girls never came. But the bugs did. He got lots of bites.

Gabe knew about the girls' meeting place. They must have changed it.

Finally Gabe gave up and went home. He hardly slept all night. His bites itched.

30

The next day, the Koots met after school at Gabe's house. Gabe had called the meeting to see what new clues there were. Nobody had anything.

"Well, I have something," Gabe said at last. He rubbed his arms. The bug bites still itched.

"I found this note yesterday." He passed the note around.

"Last night, I staked out the trailer park. They never showed up. It seems funny that they were going to meet by the I L♥ve Elvis sign. I think they are the fan club."

"Who are **they?**" asked Ty.

"Pam, Anna, Jamie, Jade, and Sara," explained Gabe.

"Oh, them," said all the other Koots.

"Pam lives in the trailer court. Maybe that was just an easy place for them to meet," said Toby.

"Maybe so. Maybe not," said Gabe. "Maybe they were going to have a fan-club meeting."

"Well, we can spy on them and see if they do anything funny," said Ben.

"They are all weird," said Ty. "They're just the kind of weird people who would do this."

"But is their writing good enough?" asked Abe. "I sure can't write that well."

"Then you don't know girls, Abe," said Gabe. "Girls love to write. They even like to practice their writing. I think girls made the signs. Don't you guys?"

All the Koots agreed.

"Here's the deal," said Toby. "Anna sits close to me at school. I'll keep an eye on her."

"I'll watch Sara," said Abe. "She lives at the apartments. And she's in my class."

"I don't want anything to do with any girl," said Ty. He looked around. The other Koots stared at him.

"Okay, okay. I'll watch Jade when we're in class. But I won't follow her home," said Ty.

"Mostly just see if they pass any more notes," said Gabe.

"I guess I could spy on Jamie," said Ben.

That left Pam for Gabe to check on.

Chapter 6

The Spies

Gabe had another idea too. He had thought up a plan while he watched the I L♥ve Elvis sign. But he kept this a secret from the other Koots.

The Boys-and-Girls Club was holding its yearly talent show. It would be a week from Friday. Gabe had signed up.

He got a fancy shirt from one of his sisters. He made a guitar out of a cardboard box. His mom helped him find some music. He practiced and practiced.

Meanwhile, the Koots watched the girls.

After school, Jamie and Jade were walking home. They turned around. Ben was right behind them. He was so close that he could hear them talking. But not so close that he could touch them.

"What are you doing, you cootie?" asked Jamie.

"Walking home," said Ben. "Just like you. I have a right to walk on this sidewalk."

"Well, stay away from us," said Jade. "You're too close. We don't want your cooties!"

Ben just smiled.

The girls stopped.

"You walk in front of us," said Jamie. "I don't trust you back there."

"Ladies before gentlemen," said Ben. He made a little bow.

"Over my dead body," said Jamie. "You go first."

"If I must," said Ben. He walked past the girls. Then he walked so slowly they could hardly move.

"Oh, forget it," Jamie said finally.

She and Jade passed Ben. To get away from him, they ran the rest of the way home. Ben just laughed.

The next day, Toby saw Anna give something to each of her friends. He told the Koots.

"Anna just gave all the girls something. See, Pam is reading it."

The Koots turned toward the girls.

"I bet Anna is having a party," said Ben. "I bet it's her birthday."

"Let's find out," said Abe.

"How?" asked Gabe. "They won't tell us."

"We don't know that until we ask them," said Toby. "Go ahead, Abe. Ask them."

Abe walked over to the girls.

"Hi," he said. "Are you having a birthday party, Anna?"

"Girls only, cootie," said Anna. "It's none of your business."

"Scram, cootie!" yelled Jamie. "Leave us alone!"

Abe came back to the safety of his friends. "Those girls sure aren't very friendly," he said.

The rest of the Koots just laughed. They had already learned that lesson.

Chapter 7

The Invitation

That afternoon, Ty and Abe walked home from school. As they got close to the apartments, Abe saw something on the ground. He picked it up. It was a note about a party. It said

Please come to my birthday party.

When: Friday night at 6:30

Where: Skate South

Your friend, Anna

"This is what we saw Anna give her friends," said Abe. "The party is Friday night at Skate South."

"I don't know," said Ty. "This could be a trick. Let's show it to the other Koots."

Later, the Koots met by the I L♥ve Elvis sign in front of the trailer court. The chalk was getting messed up. The sign was becoming hard to read. And the Koots hadn't solved the mystery yet.

Ty and Abe showed the other Koots the note.

"I think this is a fake," said Gabe. "They want us to go to Skate South. Then they'll go somewhere else."

41

"I think it's real," said Abe. "My little sister Kim walked home behind Anna today. She said Anna was talking about going skating Friday."

"And none of us were around to hear," said Ben. "I bet they'll be at Skate South Friday night."

"It would be a good chance to spy on them," said Toby. "We could skate behind them. And we could bug them."

"What if they're not there?" asked Gabe.

"We'll have fun anyway," said Ben.

Friday night at 6:30, all the Koots were at Skate South. They stayed there until Gabe's dad picked them up at 9:30. They didn't get a chance to spy on the girls. The girls never showed up.

42

Chapter 8

The Girls

Early Saturday morning, the Koots called a meeting. They met at Ben's trailer.

"Did you guys check out the I L♥ve Elvis signs?" asked Ty. "They've been fixed. I know those girls did it last night. And they got us to go to Skate South so we'd be out of their way."

"I bet Anna had an overnight for her birthday," said Ben.

"I know where she lives," said Toby. "Let's go see."

The Koots walked the block to Anna's house. When they got there, the girls were just leaving. The Koots sat on the curb across the street. They watched the girls come out of the house.

The girls came out carrying blankets and pillows and sleeping bags. They carried other things too. They had half-eaten bags of chips and girl stuff like hair things and makeup. They all looked very tired. Anna waved good-bye from her doorway. She stood on one foot. Her left foot was bandaged.

Pam looked across the street. "What are you cooties looking at?" she yelled.

"What happened to Anna?" asked Ben.

"None of your business!" Pam yelled back.

"She stepped on some glass yesterday," yelled Sara.

"What else do you want to know, nosy?" asked Jamie.

"Do you love Elvis?" asked Gabe.

"Who?" yelled Jade.

"Elvis. Do you love Elvis?" yelled Gabe.

"You're weird," yelled Pam. "And keep your cooties on that side of the street!"

Chapter 9

Back to Square One

"I don't think the girls had anything to do with Elvis," said Abe. "I think Anna hurt her foot, so they changed the party plans."

"So now we're back to square one again," said Toby. "We still don't know who loves Elvis."

"We don't know anything more than we did a week ago," said Ty. "This is really bugging me."

"Me too," said Abe, Toby, and Ben.

"I think I have another lead," said Gabe. He pulled a piece of paper from his pocket. He spread it out in front of his friends. It was an ad for a look-alike Elvis. He was coming to town next weekend.

"Where did you get this?" asked Toby.

"My mom picked it up at the Stop 'n Shop," said Gabe.

"Maybe those chalk drawings are ads for him," said Ben.

"That's just what I was thinking," said Gabe. "I wish we could go see him. But it costs ten bucks."

48

"Even if I had ten bucks, I wouldn't spend it to see a fake Elvis," said Ty.

"Besides, he's on the same night as the Boys-and-Girls Club talent show," said Gabe.

"Yeah! And that's free," said Ben.

"And who knows," said Gabe. "Maybe Elvis will be there."

"Fat chance," said Toby.

"Let's try to find out more about this guy," suggested Ben. "We could call the number for tickets. They might tell us something."

The people at the ticket office weren't much help. The Koots asked Mrs. Purdy too. They tried everything they could think of. But no one knew anything about the look-alike Elvis.

Chapter 10

Elvis Appears

The next week went by slowly. Anna came to school on Monday. But she had a little limp.

At last, Friday night came. It was time for the Boys-and-Girls Club talent show.

The Koots went without Gabe. He told them he had to go with his family.

Everybody was there. Most of the kids from school. Many of the grown-ups who lived nearby. And a few people from far away.

The show began. A man with a mike came onstage. He said, "Good evening, ladies and gentlemen. Tonight we have some very good acts. And we have prizes for the two best acts.

"First prize is a VCR," the man continued. "Second prize is a new CD player. Both prizes are given by Sounds Plus. Let's give Sounds Plus a big hand."

Everybody clapped.

The first act was a group of kids singing about the Old West. The second act was a lively tap dance number.

There were ten acts in the show. Number ten was Gabe.

Finally, it was Gabe's turn. The man with the mike said, "And now, last but not least, I'm happy to present Elvis!"

The crowd went, "Ooooohhhhh!"

Gabe ran out onto the stage. He had on his Elvis shirt. A scarf hung around his neck. His hair was combed back. His guitar made from a cardboard box looked almost real.

The music started playing. Gabe mouthed the words. He sang "Don't Be Cruel." The crowd clapped and clapped. Then he sang "Hound Dog." He finished with "Jailhouse Rock." He danced around. He wiggled his hips. At the end of the songs, he got down on one knee.

Then Gabe pulled the scarf from
his neck. He threw it out to the
crowd. Mrs. Purdy made a grab for it
and got it.

53

The crowd went wild. Gabe had been almost as good as the real Elvis.

The tap dancers won first prize. But Gabe won second prize. He now owned a new CD player.

The Koots were shocked. They didn't even know Gabe had been thinking of this. After the show, they gathered around him.

"Good work, man!" shouted Ben.

"Way to go!" said Ty.

"So you're the look-alike Elvis!" said Toby.

"I guess Elvis was here after all," said Abe.

Gabe's mom ran up and gave him a big hug. Then each of his five older sisters gave him hugs.

Next came Mrs. Purdy. She gave him a kiss on the cheek. "That was great, honey," she said. "You make the cutest little Elvis I ever saw!" Gabe's face got red.

Then Pam, Anna, Jade, Sara, and Jamie walked up.

Pam said, "Well, I hope you're proud of yourself. You've wrecked our Elvis club! We were the youngest Elvis fan club in the country too."

"Now we don't even like Elvis. All because of you," said Sara.

Jade said, "We just knew if you found out, you cooties would wreck it for us."

"So you **did** write the I L♥ve Elvis signs!" said Abe.

55

"Did you really hurt your foot, Anna? Or did you just want us out of the way so you could fix your Elvis signs?" asked Ben.

"None of your cootie business!" said Anna. The girls all put their arms around each other. They marched off. Anna didn't limp anymore.

The Koots watched them go. They just smiled. Another case solved!